CW01022801

Jake's Journey

– GREGOR GIRVAN –

Printed and bound in England by www.printondemand-worldwide.com

http://www.fast-print.net/bookshop

Jake's Journey
Copyright © Gregor Girvan 2018

Illustrations by Ali Moreton.

A catalogue record for this book is available from the British Library

ISBN 978-178456-568-8

First published 2018 by
FASTPRINT PUBLISHING
Peterborough, England.

JAKE'S JOURNEY

Bear Words

groddle – human (man or woman)

grout – bad human

A New Day

Jake was the last to leave the team bus. Without thinking he stepped down, somehow missed his footing and dropped to the pavement like a lumpy dumpling.

He got up quickly, hoping that none of his team-mates had noticed. That wasn't the case, however.

'Nice move,' said Ray, 'Perhaps a forward roll to follow,' he joked.

Jake was used to such teasing. Ever since he could remember, he'd been prone to bumping into doors, falling over, or dropping things.

Jake ran over to his pal and said, 'You know I'm practising to be a stunt bear.' Ray turned to Jake and gave him a wry smile.

Start Of The Journey

A few days later, The Ready Bears boarded a plane to America. It was the first time Jake had returned to his homeland; he was excited, but a little fearful too.

Jake entered the cabin and looked to where Ray was sitting. His pal was wearing glasses, which made him look brainy but sometimes led to teasing from the other Bears. He liked and admired Ray, as he was honest and didn't do things just to be popular or fit in with the latest fashion.

'All set, buddy?' said Ray enthusiastically, as his friend took a seat beside him.

'Well, yeah, I've never played against bison before,' Jake replied. 'I've heard they're very powerful and are prone to leaving poo all over the pitch… maybe there'll be a lot of slide tackling,' he chuckled.

Jake chatted away about football, but Ray sensed his pal was avoiding the subject which concerned him… guns.

Ray spoke up. 'If we come across a groddle with a gun, how will you feel?'

'I don't know; I've never seen anyone with a gun in Scotland, so I don't know how I'll react in the USA,' Jake replied quietly.

'Try to remember that most groddles who carry guns won't be grouts,' Ray assured him.

Jake smiled back at his wise little friend. It was a long flight ahead, but he was glad to have Ray at his side and the two friends chatted happily over a meal before nodding off.

Ray awoke as the plane landed. He waited for a few moments before stirring his friend, who groaned loudly as he came to. Jake was a grizzly bear all right, not just in name.

An hour later, The Ready Bears made their way through Customs into the arrivals hall. Ray was chatting to some of his team-mates when he noticed that Jake had stopped and was staring at two groddles. He could see they were policemen, and both were wearing holsters with guns. As he got closer he couldn't believe his eyes. The guns seemed to have disappeared and orange goo started to slide through the holsters and down the legs of the groddles.

Without thinking, Ray put his arm round Jake and led him away from the groddles towards the exit doors. Ray could hear the commotion behind him, but he didn't look back; instinctively, he knew his friend had been the cause of the mysterious goo.

Outside the building, the two friends stood together in silence. Soon they were joined by Luigi, The Ready Bears coach.

'Hey, that was weird what happened in there,' Luigi exclaimed. 'But not to worry, our bus is over there… follow me.'

As he picked up his bags, Ray looked through the airport window. At first he thought his eyes were deceiving him. But no, not far away was another groddle, yelling and waving his arms about as orange goo slid from beneath his coat and onto the floor. A bewildered Ray quickly made his way to the bus.

Ray Figures It Out

The next day, after training, Ray noticed Jake walking towards the hotel. He ran over to his pal and put his arm around him.

'The incident at the airport yesterday was quite scary. I can't help but think that maybe you had something to do with it?' Ray enquired.

Jake looked at his little friend and wondered if all sun bears were as clever as Ray.

'I think I must have,' mused Jake before continuing, 'I remember approaching the two police groddles and, when I saw the guns, I froze. I stared at the guns and found myself repeating, "What can I do? … guns to goo".'

'And then the orange stuff started seeping down their legs?' asked Ray.

'I guess so,' Jake replied.

'Well there's more,' said Ray, 'There was another groddle who was impacted in the same way. He too had goo running down his leg. Maybe, when you were focusing on the guns, it also affected anyone nearby who had a gun,' Ray suggested.

'You mean the other groddle could also have had a gun?' Jake queried.

'Exactly… maybe you have a power which eliminates guns and identifies those who are carrying them. And, if that is the case, it appears that you can disarm groddles even if the weapons are hidden,' Ray continued.

'Jings,' exclaimed Jake, 'Could I really do that?'

'Let's get a good night's rest and we'll see what tomorrow brings,' said Ray, as he led his pal towards the hotel

Lying in bed, Jake thought about what Ray had said. If, indeed, he had such power, how and when should he use it? Jake wrestled with the duvet as he tried to pin down an answer.

Jake Reacts

The following day after training, the Bears were given time off to relax. Ray and Jake decided to visit the countryside and took a two-hour bus ride to a region known for it's natural beauty and wildlife. As they wandered through some woods, a loud bang rang out ahead of them. Running towards where the noise had come from, Jake came into a clearing and saw a herd of bison disappearing into the distance. Ray followed quickly behind and pointed to a lone bison that appeared to be caught up in the undergrowth.

A few moments later they noticed a groddle, with a raised gun, walking towards the trapped bison. Jake knew this was a grout hunting and he had to be stopped.

'Gun to goo, gun to goo,' willed Jake and, before the grout could pull the trigger, orange slime filled the grout's hands and trickled down the sleeves of his jacket. On seeing the bears and feeling the goo, the grout shrieked and ran off towards his pick-up truck.

The two bears made their way towards the stranded bison, who was gradually freeing himself from the bushes.

'Are you OK?' asked Ray.

'Yeah… I'm fine now,' the bison replied. 'I don't know how you stopped the grout… but thanks anyway.'

Jake and Ray smiled back in return.

'By the way, my name's Benny,' the bison shouted, as he galloped off to catch up with his herd.

Jake turned to his pal and shook his head. 'The grout would have left the bison where it fell and probably taken a photo of it to show others… how can shooting a defenceless animal be sport?'

'I don't know, there's a lot I don't understand about groddles and grouts,' Ray added, 'But I think that's more than enough excitement for one day, let's head back.'

Walking back to the bus stop, the two Bears came across a female groddle and a wee groddle who was crying loudly and stamping his feet. Jake was the first to notice the orange slime on his jacket.

'What happened?' Jake asked the groddle.

'I don't know,' she said, as she shrugged her shoulders. 'My son was playing with his toy gun and the next thing I knew he was wiping this orange goo on his jacket. I've no idea where the gun has gone.'

'How strange, but he seems to be OK and I'm sure the jacket will be fine after a wash,' said Ray, trying to play down the incident before ushering Jake away.

As the two pals walked together, Ray spoke up.

'You know what this means,' he whispered. 'When you use your power, it affects not just the gun you're concentrating on, but any other guns in the area. The wee groddle was probably a mile away from us when you used it to save Benny. It also explains what happened at the airport.'

Jake peered into Ray's spectacled eyes; he knew his pal's assessment was right.

After a few minutes, Jake spoke up. 'I've been thinking about my mum and what she'd have thought about how I can stop guns being used.'

'And…?' Ray replied.

'She'd be happy,' Jake answered, with a tearful smile.

Ray put his arm round his pal's shoulder as they continued towards the bus stop.

Too Much Poo

Match day arrived and The Ready Bears ran out onto the pitch of the Boston Bison. The crowd cheered and Jake looked around at the opposition. The Bison were big and looked powerful. Jake knew this would be a tough match.

Halfway through the first half, the first real chance came to The Ready Bears. A pass from Chi, the captain, split the Bison's defence and Jake rushed through, collecting the ball in his stride but, as he entered the penalty box and readied himself to shoot, his feet disappeared from under him and he crashed to the ground.

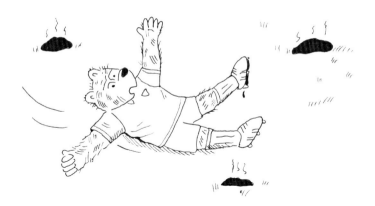

Jake rolled over and then looked at his left boot. The studs were full of poo. He gazed around the pitch to see lots of poo piles. The report about bison having leaky bottoms had been right.

The game had to go on, though, in spite of all the slipping and sliding and, just before half time, following a goalmouth scramble, The Bison scored.

As they exited the tunnel for the second half, Jake was determined to claw back a goal and found himself immediately involved in the action. He ran forward to tackle a Bison player but slipped and completely mis-timed his challenge. He heard the bison's yell of pain when he made contact, and leapt to his feet to apologise but, as he stood over the injured player, two other bison came towards him. They were bellowing in anger and lowered their horns, preparing to attack... Jake braced himself - this would be painful.

The injured bison struggled to his feet, however, and stood in front of Jake. He looked towards his angry team-mates and hollered, 'It's OK, he didn't mean that tackle.'

On hearing their team-mate's shout, the irate bison raised their heads and then moved slowly away. Jake looked at the injured bison.

'It's me, Benny,' the bison explained.

Jake was taken aback and blurted out, 'I didn't recognise you.'

'How could you forget this handsome head?' said Benny, pointing.

Jake smiled. ' Well... I must have been dazzled by your beauty,' and he jogged back into position.

The match resumed and, ten minutes from time, The Ready Bears equalised with a great shot from Jock. The game finished all square, which the TV commentators felt was a fair result.

As they left the pitch, Benny trotted over to Jake.

'Just wanted to say thanks again... who would have thought a bear would come to the rescue of a bison?' Benny remarked.

'Maybe that's the future - animals sticking together to stop grouts destroying us and our planet,' Jake replied.

Benny grinned and shouted, 'Animals United, that really would be an unbeatable team', waving goodbye as he raced off to join his team mates.

The next day, The Ready Bears travelled to New York and spent a few hours sightseeing. Jake loved the yellow taxis but couldn't understand why groddles built tall buildings and lived on top of one another. Maybe they were related to termites, he thought to himself.

Making their way through the airport later in the day, Ray noticed that, as before, Jake had stopped in front of two armed policemen. Ray stared in anticipation... what would happen? But after a few moments, and without any incident, Jake continued walking; he was whistling one of Elvis McMeaty's favourite songs. As he did so, Ray gave a deep sigh of relief, pleased that his pal's journey in overcoming his fear seemed to be complete.

Back Home

When they arrived back in Glasgow, there was a group of fans at the airport to greet the team. One of them, carrying an autograph book, rushed towards Jake. Ray sped to the side of his pal, thinking he may need some help but, surprisingly, there was no need.

Jake took the book and asked, 'Who will I write best wishes to?'

'Could you say "Follicle Fred", please, that's what my mates call me,' the groddle said, removing his hat.

'Sure will, I've always liked boiled heads,' Jake replied.

'Don't you mean bald?' the groddle asked, scratching a somewhat shiny head.

Jake laughed and said, 'Yeah, only teasing,' as he turned and winked at Ray

The next day, Jake sprang out of bed, accidently knocking over a glass of water that he'd left on the floor. Despite the mishap, he felt good and reflected on what had happened in America. He'd enjoyed going back to his homeland but decided he must look to the future. With no training until lunchtime, he switched on the TV, hoping to catch up on the football results.

The News was on and, following a couple of stories, he noticed the next item featured a report on the build-up of weapons around the world. Jake watched intently as huge guns and missiles were paraded. His initial reaction was one of despair, wondering how groddles could be so 'blobby-brained' but, a few moments later, his face gradually lit up as he looked at the TV. He stared again at the guns and then said slowly to himself, 'I wonder? ………….. maybe my journey has only just begun…'

*Other books in **The Ready Bears** series are:*

❀ A Trial For Iris
❀ Rusty's Dilemma

The Club Code

✓ *Play fair, you're a Ready Bear*

✓ *Don't dive, cheats won't thrive*

✓ *Respect the ref. he's not deaf*

✓ *Don't waste time, it's a crime*